PONY ♥ GIRLS
Kianna

By Lisa Mullarkey
Illustrated by Paula Franco

Calico

An Imprint of Magic Wagon
abdopublishing.com

To John: Husband extraordinaire and brainstorming buddy. I love you! —LM

To Mora and Mi, my dearest friends. —PF

abdopublishing.com

Published by Magic Wagon, a division of ABDO, PO Box 398166, Minneapolis, Minnesota 55439. Copyright © 2016 by Abdo Consulting Group, Inc. International copyrights reserved in all countries. No part of this book may be reproduced in any form without written permission from the publisher. Calico™ is a trademark and logo of Magic Wagon.

Printed in the United States of America, North Mankato, Minnesota.
092015
012016

 **THIS BOOK CONTAINS RECYCLED MATERIALS**

Written by Lisa Mullarkey
Illustrated by Paula Franco
Edited by Heidi M.D. Elston, Megan M. Gunderson & Bridget O'Brien
Designed by Jillian O'Brien
Art Direction by Candice Keimig

Library of Congress Cataloging-in-Publication Data

Mullarkey, Lisa, author.
  Kianna / by Lisa Mullarkey ; illustrated by Paula Franco.
    pages cm. -- (Pony Girls)
  Summary: First year camper Kianna Drake is technically too young to be a Pony Girl at Storm Cliff Stables, but in two days she will be officially eight and she is feeling homesick and a little left out, because the other Pony Girls do not seem to care.
  ISBN 978-1-62402-130-5
1. Riding schools--Juvenile fiction. 2. Camps--Juvenile fiction. 3. Horses--Juvenile fiction. 4. Birthdays--Juvenile fiction. 5. Loneliness--Juvenile fiction.
[1. Camps--Fiction. 2. Horses--Fiction. 3. Birthdays--Fiction. 4. Loneliness--Fiction.] I. Franco, Paula, illustrator. II. Title.
  PZ7.M91148Ki 2016
  813.6--dc23
  [Fic]
                    2015023274

Table of Contents

Chapter 1 ♥ **Little Miss Sunshine** ♥ 4

Chapter 2 ♥ **Care Packages** ♥ 16

Chapter 3 ♥ **The Pizza Toss** ♥ 26

Chapter 4 ♥ **Danger on the Trail** ♥ 36

Chapter 5 ♥ **Almost Eight** ♥ 49

Chapter 6 ♥ **Rainy Day Disaster** ♥ 60

Chapter 7 ♥ **No Birthday Wishes** ♥ 72

Chapter 8 ♥ **Stage Fright** ♥ 82

Chapter 9 ♥ **Kianna Rocks!** ♥ 92

Chapter 10 ♥ **Mystery Solved** ♥ 102

Chapter 1
Little Miss Sunshine

"Mail call," said Aunt Jane. "For you, Miss Daniela." She handed a thick white envelope to Dani.

Then Carly and Gabriela got even thicker ones.

I crossed my fingers. "Anything for the birthday girl?"

Carly frowned. "It's not your birthday."

I chewed my lip. "In two days it is."

Aunt Jane shuffled through her box. "I do have a postcard for a Miss Kianna Drake." She tapped her chin. "Hmm…do I know a Kianna Drake?"

"That's me!" I shouted. I grabbed the card out of her hand.

Aunt Jane isn't my real aunt. She owns Storm Cliff Stables. It's a horse camp. Everyone here calls her Aunt Jane. My mama said that if horses talked, they'd call her Aunt Jane, too.

I'm a Pony Girl. Dani, Gabriela, and Carly are Pony Girls, too. That means we're the youngest campers.

But Carly says I'm not a real Pony Girl. Real Pony Girls are eight years old. I'm only seven. But Aunt Jane let me come to camp anyway because she's friends with my mama.

I studied the postcard.

"Who's it from?" asked Dani.

"My mama." I cleared my throat and read it. "Hey, Little Miss Sunshine! Hope you're having fun in camp. Love, Mama."

Then I felt sad. I missed my mama. And my dog, Barkley. And everyone and everything else back home.

Mama said Storm Cliff Stables is only twenty miles away from home. But it's been feeling more like twenty million trillion gazillion bajillion miles away.

Aunt Jane touched my cheek. "Your mama nicknamed you Little Miss Sunshine the day you were born. You're still as sunny as ever."

I stood up taller. "I'm not so little anymore. Almost eight, you know."

"Almost," she said. "Just like every year, we'll have a nice lunch together on your birthday."

I gave Aunt Jane my sunniest smile. Then I shoved my postcard in my pocket.

Aunt Jane turned to the others before leaving. "Lots of care packages arrived today. Head down to the Green Canteen and get them."

My smile disappeared. Fast.

"What's wrong?" asked Dani.

"I hope I get one today. Especially 'cause it's…you know…my birthday."

Carly crinkled her nose. "Your birthday isn't today." Then she put her hands on her hips. "Why haven't you gotten any care packages yet?"

Dani hugged me. "I'm sure your mom sent one for your birthday."

"And for the Miss Firecracker Talent Show!" said Gabriela.

Gabriela and Dani are cousins.

I nodded. "For my birthday, I hope my mama sends me . . ."

But no one was listening. They were talking about the talent show.

I closed my eyes and made a wish. *Please let my mama send me a birthday treat and my harmonica.* I opened my eyes.

Did wishes even work without candles or stars?

"Aunt Jane said the talent show winner gets to ride any horse she wants," said Carly.

We all knew who Carly would pick.

"I'd ride Sapphire," said Carly.

Sapphire is a beautiful chestnut thoroughbred mare. Aunt Jane says she's too big for Carly to ride alone.

"If I win," I said, "I'm going to pick Queenie or Duke."

"I hope you lose," said Carly.

Gabriela flared her nostrils. "That's mean."

Carly whined. "I'm not mean! Honest! It's just my only chance to ride Sapphire." Then she grumbled.

"Even if Aunt Jane has to ride with me, it's still what I want."

Five minutes later, we were at the Green Canteen. It's a store in the Pavilion. Campers can buy all sorts of treats inside.

Mrs. Matthews was behind the counter. She clapped when she saw us. "The Pony Girls!"

She turned around to grab a stack of boxes. She set them on the counter and then turned back for even more!

"Two for Dani, four for Gabriela, and one for Carly," she said. She frowned. "Sorry, Kianna. I don't have any for you."

My eyes watered. "My mama said I'd get at least one a week."

Carly said, "Nothing again? But we've been here three weeks . . ."

Gabriela put her hand on my shoulder. "I'll share with you, Kianna."

"That's sweet of you," said Mrs. Matthews as she pointed to her computer. "Kianna, do you want to e-mail your mom and ask what happened to the packages?"

I shook my head. "No thank you. If my mama said she'd send them, then they're coming. She always tells the truth."

Carly sighed. "Not this time."

I shook my fist at Carly. "Take that back, Carly Jacobs."

Her shoulders drooped. "Sorry! Maybe she just forgot to send them."

"My mama doesn't lie or forget things." Then I remembered my postcard. Little Miss Sunshine.

I put a pretend smile on my face. "She's busy. But I'm not complaining,

Mrs. Matthews. My mama says that no one should complain at camp."

As much as I wanted a package, I wanted something else even more.

Mama.

I took my postcard out of my pocket and read it again.

If I'm supposed to be Little Miss Sunshine, how come I feel so stormy inside?

I helped the Pony Girls carry their boxes back to our cabin.

Carly opened hers first. It was a stuffed horse. She pranced it around the room. "I'm naming her Sapphire."

Dani opened hers next. The first box had butterfly earrings and a ring in it. The second box was even better.

"My butterfly wings!" she squealed. She put her arms through the little loops and fluttered around the room like a brilliant butterfly.

"These are from Abuela in Costa Rica. They're perfect for my Butterfly Dance." She put her ring and earrings on. "I hope I win the Miss Firecracker Talent Show."

Abuela is her grandmother.

Dani loves butterflies.

And Costa Rica.

And her grandmother.

Then Gabriela opened her first package.

"Is it from Abuela?" asked Dani.

Gabriela shook her head. "It's from my mom." She peered inside the box. "Nail polish, a journal, a book, and smelly pencils."

I heart smelly pencils.

Gabriela pushed the box toward me. "I want you to have these."

"Really? The smelly pencils?" I said. "Thank you so much! There are enough for all of us. We can share."

Dani stopped fluttering. She took off her ring. "You can have this, too."

"Really?" I asked. I felt like it was already my birthday!

I snatched it back. "If you don't want it, that's okay."

Gabriela's eyes lit up, so I gave her Carly's.

"It's beautiful!" said Gabriela. "I've never seen a heart-shaped rock before." She put down her box. "Can I come with you? We could get a whole bunch and paint them."

My mama would say that was a gem of an idea.

We pretended to ride horses all the way down to the barn. Bree was milking Daisy when we got there.

"Need help?" I asked.

She patted Daisy. "Always."

Bree is thirteen. She helps Aunt Jane take care of the animals. She wants to be a vet when she grows up.

"Where is everyone?" she asked.

"Opening up care packages," I said. "I didn't get one."

"Are you waiting for something special?" Bree asked.

I nodded. "My harmonica. I need it for the Miss Firecracker Talent Show. Otherwise I just don't know what I'll do for my talent."

"If you don't get it in time, you could tell jokes instead," she said. "Or you could sing or dance."

"Dani's dancing," I said, "with butterfly wings. Carly's practicing blowing bubbles with gum."

Bree laughed. "Now I know why she chews so much gum." She faced Gabriela. "What about you?"

Gabriela shrugged. "Besides riding horses, I don't really have a talent."

"That's not true," I said. "Dani says you're good at everything."

Gabriela blushed. "Not really."

I sat next to Daisy on a stool. Then I remembered the rocks. "We're going to get some of those heart-shaped rocks out back. I want one for my rock collection. But we're going to get a whole bunch and paint them."

Bree examined the rock. "I've seen these rocks. They're pretty." She put down her pail and rubbed Daisy's belly. "How about I come with you? Then maybe we can find you a harmonica."

When we walked around back, Gabriela bent down and scooped up a few rocks. "Hearts are my favorite shape."

Then my eyes lit up. But not because I saw hearts.

It was because I saw circles!

And those circles were giving me an idea. A Miss Firecracker Talent Show idea!

Chapter 3
The Pizza Toss

"Whose Hula-Hoops are those?" I asked. They were hanging on hooks.

"Aunt Jane's," said Bree. "She bought them for the vaulters. Esha has been using one during her lessons."

Last week we learned that vaulting is an equestrian sport. It's sort of like dancing and doing gymnastics on the back of a horse. While it's moving. I'm too scared to try it.

But Carly isn't. She loves it!

"Do you think Carly has used one?" I asked.

"Nope," said Gabriela. "She would have told us."

Bree picked one up. "It must be hard to balance on a horse and hula-hoop at the same time."

I ran my finger along the smooth plastic hoop. "I have an idea."

I lifted a red hoop off of the hook. I pulled it down over my head and held it around my waist. Then I pushed my hip and belly forward and swung the hoop. "Since I don't have a harmonica, I could hula-hoop for the talent show."

Gabriela sighed. "You could. But it's kinda boring just watching a hoop move round and round."

"I think it's a good idea," said Bree. "Especially if you play music while doing it."

I stopped moving my hips. The hoop fell to the ground. "If it just went round and round, that would be boring." I grabbed another hoop. "But I can do a lot more than that.

I can put one on my waist and one around my neck at the same time. Like this."

I was able to spin them both super quick.

Gabriela clapped. "You're good at this! Can you teach me?"

I dropped both hoops. "Sure! I can teach you lots of tricks. I love hula-hooping!"

"Let me try," said Bree. "I haven't used one in a long time."

She picked out an orange hoop and tried to wiggle it around her waist. It fell straight to the ground. She tried again and again. Finally, she put it back. "I was never any good at this."

"Just do what I do," I said. I lifted the orange hoop back off the hook. "Don't give up. My mama says you should never give up."

After a few minutes, they did it! Their hoops stayed up!

"Want to see another trick?" I asked. "It's my favorite one." I raised one hoop above my head. "It's called the Vortex. It looks like a barber pole that you see at barber shops."

The hoop moved up and down in a twisty position without stopping.

"The faster it moves, the cooler it looks," said Bree.

I felt like a star. A Hula-Hoop star!

"Do you know any other tricks?" asked Gabriela.

Without stopping, I yelled out, "You betcha! Here's Hooping in Lasso."

They clapped again. But this time, they clapped faster!

"Want to see a Pizza Toss?" I asked. "It is very tricky." I started with the Vortex. Next, I threw the hoop up into the air like a pizza. Then I caught it and put it back around my body without stopping.

Bree and Gabriela yelled out, "Do it again!"

So I did!

Then I grabbed three hoops and kept them spinning on my arms and leg at the same time.

When I got tired, I let the hoops crash to the floor. Then I bowed.

"Bravo!" yelled Bree.

"That's the coolest thing I've ever seen!" said Gabriela. "You must

practice a lot. It would take me forever to learn all that!"

"My mama and I started playing with a hoop at Field Day in kindergarten. I wasn't good at first. But I practiced a lot."

I put the hoops back on the hook.

"How did you learn the harder tricks?" asked Gabriela.

I laughed. "Gabriela! You should know. What are you always doing?"

"Reading," she said. "So you learned it from a book?"

I nodded. "And I watched videos online. Maybe my mama will let me post a video when I go home."

And when I posted my video, I planned to be wearing the Miss Firecracker Talent Show medal around my neck!

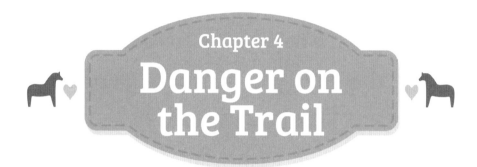

Chapter 4
Danger on the Trail

I told the other Pony Girls my big news at lunch. "If I don't get my harmonica, I'll do Hula-Hoop tricks in the show."

Carly blew a bubble. "Aren't Hula-Hoops sort of babyish?"

My mama said to ignore rude people. So I ignored her.

Layla walked over. "Gabriela, your jumping lesson's starting."

Carly cracked her gum. "I'm vaulting today." She shoved more gum into her mouth and left with Gabriela.

Layla glanced down at her clipboard. "Looks like you two are hitting the trails with me."

Dani flapped her arms. "I saw the most *beautiful* butterfly last time. Rolling Hills is the best trail here."

Layla laughed. "It's the only trail you've been on! Until today."

"Are we going to High Point?" I asked. "Or Crestview Mountain?"

Layla covered her heart with her hands. "No way! You're not ready for those yet. But you're both ready for Mountain Creek."

"Just the two of us?" I asked.

Dani spoke up. "The other girls can't come because..."

Layla interrupted. "They have other activities today."

When we got to the stable, Bree had already tacked up the horses.

Five minutes later, with Layla's help, I mounted Sunburst. Dani rode Duke.

Layla led the way through the winding woods. "Keep your ears and eyes open. You never know what you'll run into on a trail. There's lots to look at of course. But take a few minutes just to listen. You'll be surprised at what you'll hear."

Just then, a monarch butterfly fluttered by Dani's head. She watched it as it danced around Duke's ears.

Dani spoke calmly. "See, Layla? I'm learning. The first time we were out, I saw a fox on the trail and I screamed. Remember I spooked Blue?"

"How could I forget?" said Layla. "But look at you now. You're both sitting tall in your saddles and leading your horses. You're not letting them lead you anymore."

I looked back at Dani. "If you see another fox, don't scream. Remember to stay calm. If you're calm, your horse will be calm, too."

Dani frowned. "I didn't scream because I was scared the other day. I was just excited."

"We know," said Layla. "But Kianna's advice is a smart reminder."

Dani rubbed Duke's neck. "I won't forget."

We rode about a half mile without talking. That was hard to do, especially because I wanted to talk about my birthday!

Finally, I couldn't take it anymore. "So what sounds did everyone hear?"

Layla spoke first. "I heard bees buzzing, water from a brook or stream, and a woodpecker. At least I think it was a woodpecker. Someone sneezed, too."

"That was me," said Dani, smiling.

"And oddly enough," said Layla, "I heard someone humming 'Happy Birthday.'"

I giggled. "Guilty. My birth—"

But then Layla put up her hand and pulled back the reins on her horse.

She pointed to a raccoon about ten feet away.

"He's so cute!" I said. I wanted to see it up close so I slid off of Sunburst.

Layla jumped off her horse and lifted me into the air before I knew

what was happening. Then she pushed me down onto my saddle.

She looked scared. She breathed heavy as she ran back to her horse and got back on.

She hissed at me, "What were you thinking, Kianna? Don't ever get off your horse on a trail without permission. Plus, raccoons are not supposed to be out during the day."

The raccoon was having trouble walking. "He looks hurt," I said.

"He probably has rabies," said Dani.

I wasn't sure what rabies were, but I knew it must be something bad. Real bad.

The raccoon looked up at us but didn't move.

Layla's voice got cranky. "Aunt Jane is going to pitch a fit when she finds out."

I tried to say I was sorry, but Layla held up her hand. It was shaking. "Lead your horses in a straight line down the trail. This is no time for them to get spooked by a sick raccoon of all things."

I looked straight ahead and led my horse down the path. Dani did too. A few minutes later, we were in an open field. Layla said, "We can stop and let the horses rest. We're safe."

Then she used her grouchy voice again. "Kianna, you're never to approach *any* wild animal. You should know that by now! I'm disappointed you forgot that rule so easily."

I felt the opposite of sunshiny.

Layla rubbed her temples. "It's time to head on back now."

When we finally got back to the stalls and dismounted, we checked under the horses' saddle pads just like Bree said to do to make sure they sweated evenly.

"Is there a section that has more sweat than the other parts?" she asked.

"All even," I said.

"Mine too," said Dani.

"Good job," said Bree. "Then there's no need to adjust the saddles."

Layla glared at me. "But we do need to adjust the behavior of some campers." Then she walked out of the barn without saying good-bye.

I wanted to jump back on Sunburst and ride her all the way home.

Layla still seemed upset with me at the campfire later. I waved to her, but she hardly smiled back. Then she marched over to Aunt Jane.

"Layla's still mad at me," I said.

Dani shrugged. "Why do you say that?"

I pointed to her and Aunt Jane. They were opening marshmallow bags and talking. "Because she just pointed over here at me. She had her cranky face on and was using that grouchy voice."

"What did she say?" asked Carly.

"I don't know," I said. "I can't hear her from all the way over there."

Carly laughed. "Then how do you know she's using her grouchy voice?"

"I just know, that's all. When I waved to her and Aunt Jane, they didn't wave back."

Gabriela looked over at them. "They do kinda look mad about something."

Carly agreed. "They could be upset that we're running out of marshmallows. I heard them say that they should have gotten more."

"Really?" I asked. "Because that makes me feel a whole lot better if it's true."

And it must have been true because a minute later, Aunt Jane and Layla were laughing.

I felt better. So much better that I walked over and picked out a stick. Even though somehow I could not get the hang of roasting marshmallows.

"Here's a long one for you," said Jaelyn, Bree's friend. "Don't forget to push the marshmallow down on the stick a little bit more. You don't want it to fall into the fire again."

But it did fall in the fire. Every single time I tried to make one.

"You're holding it over the fire too long," said Jaelyn. She held her stick high above the fire.

"But if you don't touch the fire," I asked, "how are you gonna toast it?"

"Just watch," said Esha.

I watched. But nothing happened.

"What am I watching?"

Esha rolled her eyes. "Listen Pony Girl, just watch the marshmallow. You'll see."

So I watched Jaelyn twirl the marshmallow high above the fire. It was boring. Until I noticed it getting a little brown. And then it got darker and darker.

Jaelyn backed away from the fire.

"Hey, it worked," I said. "It's toasty."

Jaelyn grabbed a graham cracker. She broke it in half and put some chocolate on one half. Then she sandwiched the marshmallow, squeezed, and slowly slid it off the stick.

When she squished her s'more together, toasty, gooey marshmallow leaked out every side. "Perfection!" she said.

"What next?" I asked.

"Eat it," said Esha. "What else?"

Jaelyn took a huge bite. "Your turn. Remember to keep it above the fire."

For the next twenty minutes, the Pony Girls toasted marshmallows. I felt like an eight-year-old already!

We were having so much fun until
Aunt Jane walked over.

"Want one, Aunt Jane?" I asked.

But Aunt Jane didn't want a s'more. She wanted to talk.

"Kianna, I just spoke to Layla about your trail ride today. I allowed you to go to Mountain Creek because I thought you were ready. But being ready includes being responsible."

I suddenly felt like an ooey-gooey marshmallow.

"But now I know you weren't ready for the trail at all."

"Oh, no, Aunt Jane. I was ready! I just had a small problem, that's all."

Aunt Jane bit her lip. "Getting off your horse to approach a sick animal is a big problem."

Esha's eyes grew wide. "Even I wouldn't do that."

"You're never, ever to approach any animals in the wild," said Aunt Jane.

"I'm sorry," I said. "The raccoon was just so cute. I didn't know he was sick."

That's when Layla used her grouchy voice again. "But he *was* sick, Kianna. He could have bitten you, and then you would have been sick, too."

Carly shook her finger at me. "Remember when I tried to help Gertie?"

Gertie was a garter snake that Carly wanted to keep as a pet. It bit Bree's finger.

"That wasn't a very good idea I had," said Carly. "I learned my lesson, though."

Then Aunt Jane sort of smiled. "Your mama would be upset if I didn't keep you safe. But you have to keep yourself safe, too. Next time, make a smarter choice, okay?"

When they walked away, I heard Layla say, "She's only seven, Aunt Jane. That's the problem."

I clenched my fists. "Almost eight," I whispered. "Almost eight."

Chapter 6
Rainy Day Disaster

"What are we going to do all day in this rain?" asked Carly. "It's going to be a really boring day. B-O-R-I-N-G!"

I thought the same thing. It was only breakfast time, but I was already tired of the rain. It was an ugly day.

"Nonsense," said Aunt Jane. "This is Storm Cliff Stables. We love a good storm here every once in a while. We're prepared."

The older girls at our table started chanting. "Storm Cliff Stables! Storm Cliff Stables! Storm Cliff Stables!"

Layla stood in front of the fruit bar and spoke into the microphone. "Finish your breakfast, campers. Then pick your first activity. Everything starts in ten minutes."

A crash of thunder made Layla jump.

"We're not going to let a little rain stop us, are we?" she asked.

The chanting got louder. "Storm Cliff Stables! Storm Cliff Stables!"

Aunt Jane glanced at my plate. "Not hungry today?"

I tried to smile but I couldn't. "My tummy feels yucky." I lowered my eyes. "I can't eat when I think about that baby raccoon. He was so sick." I poked at my eggs with a fork. "I'm sorry, Aunt Jane. Please don't be mad at me."

"Today's a new day," said Aunt Jane. "I wasn't mad at you. I was concerned for you."

Then she hugged me. "How could I be mad at the birthday girl?"

"One more day," I said. "I'll finally be eight."

Carly, Gabriela, and Dani started to giggle.

"What's so funny?" I asked. "Are you laughing at me?"

"No one's laughing at anyone," said Aunt Jane. "Now get going to your first activity."

She waved good-bye.

"Let's go pick out our activity," I said.

"Oh, we're not signing up for anything," said Gabriela. She gave

Carly and Dani a quick glance. "We're working on a special project with Layla."

"What about me?" I asked.

Dani sucked in her breath.

Gabriela sighed.

Carly shook her head.

"It's something that only eight-year-olds can work on," said Dani. "Sorry."

My tummy felt like ooey-gooey marshmallows again.

Bree heard Dani. She said, "Hang out with me. I'm visiting Pip and

Squeak in a few minutes. Wanna come and help me out?"

I jumped up and down. "I love Pip and Squeak!" I stuck my tongue out at the Pony Girls. "I'd rather go with Bree anyway."

Pip and Squeak are miniature horses.

"Aunt Jane asked me to groom them before Layla does some groundwork with them," she said. "You can learn more about grooming."

We walked down to the barn. As soon as the horses saw us, they made soft neighing sounds. I picked up a carrot out of a bucket. "Can I feed them?"

Bree rubbed Pip's belly. "Sure."

I took the carrot and let Squeak nibble some of it first. Pip must have been hungry, too. She stretched out her neck and pushed Squeak out of the way.

"I think they both want a treat now," I said.

So while I fed Pip, Bree fed Squeak.

"Is Esha still trying to get on Pip and go for a ride?" I asked.

"No," said Bree. "She knows she's too big. She finally understood that she'd hurt their spines if she sat on them. Even for a second.

"Aunt Jane and Layla reminded her that the preschoolers are the only ones who have permission to ride them."

I hugged the horses and whispered, "Tomorrow is my birthday, but no one cares."

"That's not true," said Bree. "I care."

Bree is a good listener. Way better than the Pony Girls.

"It's true," I said. "I think my mama forgot. I still didn't get a care package from her. And the Pony Girls don't even want to spend time with me because I'm seven. I keep trying to tell them that I'm almost eight."

"Did they say that?" asked Bree. "That they don't want to spend time with you? That they don't care?"

"Sort of," I said. "Every time I tell them I'm almost eight, they talk about something else."

Bree gave sugar cubes to Pip and Squeak. She was quiet for a bit. Then she hugged me. "The Pony Girls do care about you. I just know it."

But *I* didn't know it. And it made my heart hurt and my tummy feel yucky.

Bree and I didn't talk much. But she did let me help her brush Pip and pick out Squeak's hooves. It was hard work.

"Now that we're done, do you want to go to the Green Canteen and see if your mama sent you a care package?"

She put her arm around my shoulder. "I have a good feeling that today is your lucky day. Your care packages are going to show up. Just wait and see!"

"Okay," I said. I crossed my fingers. Then I crossed my arms and legs for extra good luck.

But today was not my lucky day.

No care packages.

No signs of any party decorations.

No sunshine.

And worst of all, I didn't see the Pony Girls for the rest of the day.

Chapter 7
No Birthday Wishes

"Rise and shine," whispered a voice in my ear. "You know what day it is, don't you?"

I sat up in bed and yawned. "It's my eighth..."

"It's the day of the Miss Firecracker Talent Show!" Carly squealed.

"It's also my birthday," I whispered.

But I don't think anyone heard me, because no one said anything.

"We have to go to the Pavilion," said Dani. "We'll be back."

"But we always go to the Pavilion together," I said. "For breakfast. And I didn't really see you at all yesterday."

I had spent the day with Bree and her friends. I never even saw the Pony Girls.

"Sorry," said Gabriela. "Layla just needs us for a couple of minutes before we eat. Promise."

They shuffled out the door.

I got up from my bunk, brushed my teeth, and looked in the mirror.

"Happy Birthday! You're officially a Pony Girl."

A Pony Girl no one cares about, apparently.

Someone knocked on the door. It was Bree.

"Happy birthday, Kianna!"

"You remembered!" I gave her one of my superduper hugs.

She looked confused. "Of course I remembered! I want to buy you some stickers for your collection at the Green Canteen."

"Oh, boy! My first present."

Bree laughed. "It's just a small gift. I bet your mom sent you a care package today. We can check while we're there."

Because it was my birthday, Bree gave me a piggyback ride all the way there!

When I told Bree that no one else had wished me a happy birthday, she looked surprised. "Maybe they were in a hurry?"

I bit my lip and shrugged.

"It's only 8 o'clock in the morning, Kianna. Lots of people will wish you a happy birthday today. I'm just sure of it."

But I *wasn't* so sure. "It's a busy day. The talent show is today. Plus Dani, Gabriela, and Carly signed up for vaulting classes. They know I'm too afraid to go."

"There's always tonight," said Bree.

"But tonight's only a small part of today," I said. Then I thought of my mama. I was her Little Miss Sunshine. So I pushed away my sad thoughts and tried to have happy ones.

When we got to the Green Canteen, Mrs. Matthews waved. She held up a package.

"It's finally here!" I said. "My birthday gift from my mama!"

Mrs. Matthews shook her head and lowered the box. "Oh, I'm sorry, Kianna. I was hoping you could give this to Carly."

My eyes stung. "So there's no package for me? It's my birthday, you know."

"I didn't know! Happy birthday! Come back later and I'll give you

a Mango Surprise. On the house. Everyone deserves a birthday treat."

"Really?" I asked. "That's my favorite ice cream. I can't wait to tell Aunt Jane."

"Aunt Jane isn't here," she said. "Not sure if she's coming back today or tomorrow."

My heart sank. I always see Aunt Jane on my birthday. Always.

"Where is she?" asked Bree.

"Said something about having to run some errands and check on her house," said Mrs. Matthews.

The door squeaked open. It was Esha, Avery, and Jaelyn. Jaelyn was holding a paintbrush and Esha had purple paint on her face.

When they saw us, they slammed the door and quickly walked away.

"What's that all about?" asked Mrs. Matthews.

Bree threw her hands in the air. "I don't know, but it's rude. They could have said happy birthday to Kianna. They know it's her special day."

It sure didn't feel special. I sat down on a bench. "If I tell you something, can you promise to keep a secret, Bree?"

"That depends," said Bree. "If you told me that Esha wasn't wearing her helmet or a horse was left out all night, I'd have to tell Aunt Jane."

I shook my head. "Nothing like that. It's about me."

I took a deep breath. "I used to love Storm Cliff Stables. But now I don't even like it. It's not the right place for me anymore."

Then I started to cry. "I wanna go home."

Chapter 8
Stage Fright

"You can't go home now!" said Bree. "At least not today."

I blew my nose. "My mama said I could call if I needed her. I really need her now."

Bree was quiet for a minute. Then she glanced at her watch. "The talent show starts in two hours. You've worked hard. You could win! Wouldn't that be a cool present?"

"Besides my stickers and ice cream treat, it may be my only present."

"Then that settles it," said Bree. "Enter the contest. Have some fun with it. If you don't have a good time today, we can call your mama tonight. Deal?"

"Deal," I said. "But I don't want to see any Pony Girls before the contest. If I see them, I might cry."

"No problem," said Bree. "We'll hang out at the barn and practice until the show starts."

And that's just what we did.

Bree had a lot of Hula-Hoops stashed in the barn. "I've been practicing, but I'm not getting better."

She picked out the red one and handed it to me. I put it around my waist and started to make it go back and forth.

"The Vortex move is my favorite," said Bree. "Show it to me again."

"Easy peasy," I said. "The girls are going to want to do it, too."

Then I tossed the hoop up in the air. "I think they're going to like the Pizza Toss the best though. It's my favorite trick." I kept tossing the hoop up in the air and catching it. "You can only do this trick if you can do the Vortex move."

I showed Bree so many tricks that we almost missed the talent show. When we got to the Pavilion, we peeked in the side door.

There were chairs and long benches set up around the stage. I could see the Pony Girls sitting on the chairs in the first row. The stage had some potted plants and flowers on both sides. The stage looked big.

Too big. My tummy got that ooey-gooey marshmallow feeling again.

Streamers and balloons were hanging from the ceiling behind the stage. Between them, there was a big sign with red, white, and blue letters spelling out "Miss Firecracker Talent Show."

Music was blasting. Esha and Avery were dancing.

When I walked in, Carly, Gabriela, and Dani ran up to me.

"Where have you been?" asked Dani.

"We've been looking all over for you," said Gabriela.

"We looked everywhere but we couldn't find you," said Carly.

Layla looked in our direction. She spoke into a microphone. "Attention, everyone. We have a great show today. In fact, one of our acts will perform twice."

"Hey, that's not fair," I said. "They'll have double the chance of winning." But no one else seemed to mind.

For the next hour, I watched girls twirl batons, hip-hop dance, sing songs, flip through the air, and perform magic tricks.

When it was Carly's turn, she couldn't make a bubble. On her third try, the pink gum shot across the stage. Everyone laughed. Even Carly.

Then Carly popped more gum into her mouth. She chewed it and finally blew a bubble. But it was not the World's Biggest Bubble. It was the World's Smallest Bubble.

Carly stomped her foot and walked offstage. Her cheeks were pinker than her gum.

Then Layla called Dani up to the stage. Dani was a beautiful butterfly. She had sparkles everywhere.

The music started. Dani started to dance. She fluttered around the stage. The music finally stopped.

But Dani did not stop dancing. She twirled and whirled to the right. Then she twirled and whirled to the left. Finally, Layla had to ask her to twirl and whirl right back down to her seat.

Then it was my turn. I brought my Hula-Hoops up on the stage. I looked out at the audience. There were so many people. So many people looking straight at me.

I wanted to put a hoop over my head, but my hands wouldn't move. My feet wouldn't move. I had a hard

time breathing. I just kept staring at the crowd.

How was I ever going to win the contest if I was too afraid to enter it?

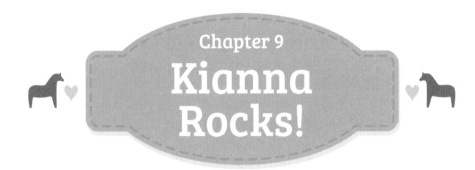

Chapter 9
Kianna Rocks!

Layla rushed over to me. "Are you okay? Do you need water?"

I shook my head. I couldn't talk. I felt like my breath had been sucked away.

"You're brave, Kianna," said Layla. "And you're eight years old now. You can do this. Believe in yourself."

Believe in yourself. That's what my mama always says to me!

I took a deep breath. I held it for a few seconds and then exhaled. Then I did it again. Then I gave Layla the thumbs-up sign. "I'm ready."

I wasn't sure I could hula-hoop in front of all the campers, but I knew I had to try.

"Fellow campers," said Layla, "be prepared to be razzle-dazzled by the Hula-Hoop Queen, Kianna Drake!"

The Pony Girls went wild! They pulled out posters with special messages from under their seats and held them up.

Go Get 'Em, Birthday Girl! Kianna Rocks! This Birthday Girl Has Talent!

Those posters made me feel better. I turned my frown upside down. Suddenly, I knew I could do it.

I stepped forward and started twirling a hoop around my waist.

The girls clapped, but not too much.

Then while one hoop spun around my waist, Bree handed me another hoop. I put it over my head and spun it around my neck.

The claps got louder.

My spinning got faster!

Next, I stuck out my leg. Bree added a smaller hoop to it.

Just like we practiced!

I twirled it round and round just like the others.

The clapping got even louder. Girls started to shout my name. Some of them got out of their seats. They rushed up to get a closer look.

When my first song ended, I let all three hoops fall to the floor.

"Do it again!" someone shouted.

The second song started.

"I'm going to show you some very tricky tricks," I shouted.

The girls clapped and cheered when I showed them the Vortex, the Pizza Toss, and Hooping in Lasso.

When I finished, I took a bow and ran offstage.

But Layla pulled me back up again. "Let's give Kianna another minute to show us a few more tricks."

So I did. I felt like a star! A superstar!

When I was done, Layla said it was time to vote for our favorite talent.

My mama says you should never vote for yourself. So I voted for Dani. Her dance was really good.

While we were waiting for the results, lots of girls grabbed a hoop and tried doing some of my tricks. One of the older campers could do all of them!

I looked around for the Pony Girls. Where were they?

But then Bree and her friends came up onstage and high-fived me.

"You're a shoo-in," said Bree. "Everyone's voting for you."

Esha nodded. "Way better than that bubblegum girl."

I crossed my fingers. "I hope so. It would be fun to win the contest on my birthday."

A few minutes later, Layla quieted everyone down. She made everyone go back to their seats. Everyone but the Pony Girls. Where were they?

"I have a special announcement," said Layla. "Although Kianna's Hula-Hoop routine is a tough act to follow, this next singing group can't be beat."

My heart sunk. Can't be beat?

"You're going to want to join them in singing this very special song," said Layla, "for a very special person."

Bree made a frowny face. "Must be the older kids. They're tough to beat, Kianna." She shrugged her shoulders. "At least you tried."

I closed my eyes. I didn't want to see the singers.

But it didn't matter, because I heard them. And what I heard made me smile. Smile a lot.

It was the bestest song ever sung by the bestest friends ever!

I opened my eyes. Carly, Dani, and Gabriela were singing "Happy Birthday." To me!

They had balloons, cards, and packages in their hands. For me!

Then Layla brought out a cake with candles on it. "There are nine candles, Kianna. One of them is for good luck."

I looked at Bree. "Today is my lucky day after all!"

I closed my eyes and made a wish.

When I opened them, I couldn't believe it! My wish had already come true!

Chapter 10
Mystery Solved

"Mama!" I shouted. I ran down the stairs and flew into her arms. "What are you doing here?"

"Happy birthday, Little Miss Sunshine! Did you think I'd miss your birthday?"

She covered my head and face with kisses.

"I'm here to have lunch with you and Aunt Jane." She held me away from her. "Let me get a better look at you." She studied me up and down. "You certainly do look older today. And I think you must have grown another inch at least since last time I saw you."

"How old do I look?" I asked.

"At least eight and a half," she said. "Maybe even eight and three-quarters."

I squeezed my mama tight.

She pointed to Jaelyn and Esha. They were hanging up a banner that said: Happy Birthday, Pony Girl!

"Looks like you've made lots of friends," she said.

I nodded. "Pony Girl, Mama! That's me! I'm officially a real Pony Girl today."

Carly, Dani, and Gabriela came running over with Bree.

"You were awesome," said Dani. "You deserve to win. I voted for you. We all did. Now you're going to have to teach us how to hula-hoop like that."

"I'd show you this afternoon, but I know you have vaulting."

Carly laughed. "No we don't. We just tried to trick you into thinking we forgot your birthday so we could surprise you."

"We made the signs yesterday. And this morning, we were helping with the cake," said Gabriela. "But then we couldn't find you and we felt awful. We were worried you thought we really *did* forget your birthday."

"Yeah," said Dani. "And you know we'd never forget that, right?"

I looked at Bree. She mouthed, "Told you so."

"Yeah," I said, "I knew you didn't forget about my birthday."

Carly tugged on Mama's shirt. "Mrs. Drake? How come you didn't send Kianna any care packages?"

Mama scrunched up her eyebrows. "What are you talking about? I think I've sent six or seven so far!"

"You have?" I asked. "I didn't get any of them! I thought you forgot all about me, Mama. I was the only one not getting packages."

Mama scratched her head. "That's strange. I brought them to the post office myself. In Bakersfield. Not to get one of them would be understandable. But not to get any of them? Something isn't right about that. I'll have to call the post office."

"No need to call," said Aunt Jane. "I solved the mystery."

Aunt Jane was pulling a squeaky-wheeled wagon in through the door. Inside were a whole bunch of boxes with brown paper on them.

"Here they are, Kianna. All seven of them," said Aunt Jane. "From your mama."

Mama looked confused.

The Pony Girls looked confused.

I must have looked confused, too.

Aunt Jane looked at Mama. "I had a funny feeling you used the same address you've been using the last 15 years to send *me* packages. Right?"

"That's right," said Mama. "That's the address I've always sent your boxes to."

"But Storm Cliff Stables has a PO Box number for packages. So the only packages we get here are the ones we pick up at the post office and bring back to camp. The boxes you sent have been sitting on my front steps for weeks! All seven of them."

Mama covered her face. "I'm so embarrassed!"

"Don't be embarrassed, Mama. I got your postcards."

"Postcards and letters come here," said Aunt Jane. "Packages don't. We have to get them ourselves and then give them out."

Then Layla's voice came booming over us. "After counting all the votes, we have a winner."

The place got quiet. Everyone rushed back to their seats.

Layla cleared her throat. "The winner of the Miss Firecracker Talent Show is . . . Kianna Drake!"

Everyone cheered.

I ran up onstage, and she put a medal around my neck. It was as glittery as Dani's butterfly wings.

"This was the best birthday ever," I said after eating lunch with Aunt Jane.

Mama hugged me. "I still feel awful. Because of my mistake, you didn't get any treats." She squeezed me extra tight. "I'm really sorry, baby."

I shrugged my shoulders. "Don't worry, Mama. A seven-year-old might get upset about that. But an eight-year-old doesn't."

I was already counting down the days until I celebrated my *ninth* birthday at Storm Cliff Stables.